SPACE BINGO

Look for these

titles, coming soon:

#2
ORBIT WIPEOUT!

#3
MONDO MELTDOWN

#4
INTO THE ZONK ZONE!

SPACE BINGO
by Tony Abbott

Illustrated by Kim Mulkey

A SKYLARK BOOK
NEW YORK·TORONTO·LONDON·SYDNEY·AUCKLAND

RL 4, 007–010

SPACE BINGO
A Skylark Book / March 1996

Skylark Books is a registered trademark of Bantam Books, a division of
Bantam Doubleday Dell Publishing Group, Inc. Registered in U.S. Patent and
Trademark Office and elsewhere.

Time Surfers is a series by
Bantam Doubleday Dell Books for Young Readers,
a division of Bantam Doubleday Dell Publishing Group, Inc.

Cover art by Frank Morris
Interior illustrations by Kim Mulkey
Cover and interior design by Beverly Leung

ISBN 0-553-48303-X

Published simultaneously in the United States and Canada.

Bantam Books are published by Bantam Books, a division of Bantam Doubleday
Dell Publishing Group, Inc. Its trademark, consisting of the words "Bantam
Books" and the portrayal of a rooster, is Registered in U.S. Patent and
Trademark Office and in other countries. Marca Registrada. Bantam Books,
1540 Broadway, New York, New York 10036.

PRINTED IN THE UNITED STATES OF AMERICA

10   9   8   7   6   5   4   3   2   1

OPM

For Patricia Reilly Giff

A great teacher, writer, and friend,
as inspired as she is inspiring

CHAPTER
1

Zzzz! Zzz—zzz!

Ned Banks huddled over the little black box on the desk in his room. He pushed away some of the switches, batteries, buzzers, and screws that were crowded around it. Then he stared at the comic book that was propped up in front of him and shook his head.

"Nope," he said to himself. "Something's just not right."

Picking up a screwdriver, he opened the back of the box.

"Ernie," he thought out loud, "I know we promised it would be tonight, but . . ." Ned

looked at his clock. "It doesn't look like I'm going to make it. Sorry, buddy."

Ernie Somers was his buddy, all right. From nursery school on. They did absolutely everything together. They'd probably be doing something right now. Except . . .

Except that Ned couldn't do things with Ernie like he usually did. Not anymore. Not since last Monday, one incredibly long week ago.

Ned and his family had moved away—way away. In fact, they had moved halfway across the country.

To a new town. A new house. And, worst of all, a new school. No more Ernie. No friends at all.

He might as well have moved to Jupiter.

Tssst! Fwing!

A blue spark shot out from the black box.

"Ned!" called a voice from downstairs. "What was that noise? What are you doing?"

"Sorry, Mom. Everything's okay!" Ned yelled, pointing the small box away from the door and toward the wall. *Gotta be more*

careful, he thought. *I'm in enough trouble already.*

When Ned had found out he was going to move, he and Ernie had made a pact.

They would find a way to talk to each other every night, just like they always did. If they couldn't do it in person, they'd decided, then it would have to be some other way.

"How about walkie-talkies?" Ernie had suggested.

"I don't know, Ern. I don't think they have the range."

"The telephone?"

"Too expensive," Ned said, shaking his head. "We're going to need something totally incredible. Something like this!"

Ned pulled his latest copy of *Ice Planet Commandos* out of his bookcase. "Look, Ern, it's right here," he said, flopping on his bed. "Zontar of Zebra Force is holding exactly what we need. A personal communicator!"

"Cool!" Ernie said, nodding. Then he frowned. "But you can't *buy* those. That's

just a drawing in a comic book."

"Hey, don't worry. I scoped it out," said Ned. "We can build them. I've already started to collect the junk we'll need. It's our only hope!"

Ernie sighed. "Yeah. Anything's worth a try. But you'd better draw me a picture so I know what to do."

That was when Ned got to work.

He started with a TV remote that nobody used anymore. He added the microphone and speaker from his sister's old tape recorder. He took the tiny lights from his train set, a paper clip for an antenna, and an electric door buzzer for a signal.

Ned told Ernie exactly how the pieces should go together. He drew detailed pictures of the communicator so that they could each build one.

"I love it," Ernie had said, examining the final product. "Everybody else will think it's all junk!"

They had a pretty good laugh about that.

But now a week had passed, and their first

official communication was supposed to happen tonight. Monday night. 7:00 P.M.

Ned hurried over to his crowded bookcase and pulled out a small plastic crate. He thought about the past week. About his totally new life. About how that life wasn't going so well.

First it was small things. Like last Monday, his first day of school. He'd dropped his lunch tray in the middle of the cafeteria. Three hundred kids had just happened to get quiet at the exact moment his tray hit the floor. Everyone had stared.

It wouldn't have been so bad except that his Thermos had exploded like a bomb and vegetable soup splattered all over him. He'd smelled like garbage for the rest of the day.

Then on Tuesday he'd caught his hair in his locker and had to ask a first-grader to help him get unstuck. "You should know better," the first-grader had kept saying. When he wasn't laughing.

Then Ned forgot his homework. Three times! Mr. Smott wouldn't even listen to

Ned's excuse the third time. He just squished his face into a horrible frown and wrote out a long note that both of Ned's parents had to sign.

And there was the screaming fight in the hall with his older sister, Carrie, when she called him Ned the Nerd. Everybody in the entire school must have heard her, because they started calling him the same thing. *Nedthenerd.* As if it was one word.

But today, today was the absolute worst. He wanted to jump into a hole and disappear.

Ned shook his head. He didn't want to think about it. He dug into the crate and pulled out a short green wire. Carefully he looped the wire around two circuit posts in the back of the communicator.

Ned couldn't wait to talk to Ernie about everything. No one else would do.

"There. Finished!" Ned said, screwing the panel back on. "Okay, Ernie," he whispered. "It's now or never."

Ned flipped a switch on the communicator

and the tiny lights flashed once. He held it up to his mouth and took a deep breath. "Ned to Ernie. Do you read me, over?"

Loud static came through the speaker.

He bent the paper clip antenna, jammed down a couple of buttons, and turned a little dial on the front.

Zzz-zzz!

The speaker began to whistle and sputter. All the little lights blinked on-off, on-off.

"Now that's more like it. Okay, Ernie, I hope you're there."

Ned put the microphone to his lips again. "Ned to Ernie. Come in."

The whistling turned to hissing, and the communicator started humming in Ned's hand.

Diddle-iddle-eep! Iddle-eep!

His desk lamp began to flicker.

"Come in," he said. "Come in!"

From out of nowhere, a burst of rushing wind whooshed through the room, ruffling Ned's hair. "Whoa! I think it's working!"

Ned stood in the middle of the floor and

braced himself. "Come in!" he shouted. "Ernie, come in!"

The whole room began to glow. The air was humming. The floor began to quake.

"Come in! Come in, come in!"

Suddenly—*WHAM!*—the door of Ned's closet blasted open. And two silver people crashed into the room at incredible speed.

"Ned!" his mother yelled. "What's that noise?"

But Ned couldn't answer.

He just watched as the two people—a boy and a girl—skidded across the floor, knocked over his small bookcase, tumbled into his desk, bounced against the bed, and landed in a heap at his feet.

Then everything went quiet.

"Well," said the boy, looking up at Ned. "You did say, 'Come in!' "

CHAPTER
2

Instantly the girl picked herself up, grabbed at her belt, and pulled off a small blinking thing. It started chirping as she waved it up and down in the air. "Scan for negative vectors," she snapped. "Now!"

The boy jumped up and did the same thing.

Ned stared at the two strangers leaping around his room. Inside, his brain was yelling, "Aliens! I've got aliens in my room! They're wearing silver suits and they're talking real funny! *HELLLLLLP!*"

But outside, all his mouth could say was, "Who . . . who . . . who . . ."

"Hmmm," said the silver boy, waving his blinking device in front of Ned. "He *looks* human, but he talks like an owl!"

Suddenly there was a sound on the stairs.

"Dive!" the girl yelled. In a flash the two strangers disappeared under the bed. Ned stood there. What was going on?

In seconds Ned's mother was in the middle of the room, staring at the floor. "Oh, Ned!" she gasped. "How can one person make such a mess?"

"But—But—" Ned stammered, looking around his room.

He wanted to tell his mother about the silver kids. About how they came from his closet and bombed his room. About how it wasn't his fault.

But his tongue felt as big as a cheeseburger.

When he could finally speak, his mother was gone. And the words ". . . cleaned up, or else!" were coming through the closed door.

When Ned turned around, they were there

again. The two silver kids. He had never seen anything like them before. He stared as they snapped the blinking devices back on their belts and looked up.

The girl had short black hair. She flashed a smile at Ned.

Was she friendly? Ned squinted back at her.

The boy started walking around Ned's room, poking and looking at things. Ned hoped he wouldn't break anything. The boy never stopped moving. He had a flattop haircut with narrow zigzags cut in the sides.

Both of them wore one-piece silver outfits, like bodysuits. And on their belts hung bunches of gadgets. Everything about these kids was blinking or buzzing or whirring.

Ned slowly shook his head from side to side. "I don't believe any of this," he mumbled. "I mean, who *are* you? *What* are you?"

The boy suddenly stopped moving, snapped his fingers, and did a short wave. "Roop!" he said.

Ned stepped back. "I knew it!" he cried.

"I knew it! You *are* an alien!"

"No," said the boy, "it's my name. Rupert Johnson. People call me Roop." The boy took a pair of green-tinted glasses from his pocket, put them on, and smiled.

"Yeah, sure," said Ned.

"I'm Suzi Naguchi," the girl said. "You're Ned, right? Isn't that what your mother called you? Well, we're TS Squad One. Greetings!"

Ned stepped back again. "Uh-huh," he said. "So what were you doing in my closet?"

The boy grinned. "We were just passing through!" He made a diving motion with his hand. "Get it? Your closet! Just passing through!" He doubled over, laughing at his own joke.

Ned wrinkled his nose.

"Sorry, Ned," said Suzi. "Roop's a real comedian. The truth is, we were in our surfie, cruising past the Sky Rink, when a bloogball slammed our space-time integrator. We lost control, flopped into a timehole, picked up a strange signal, and here we are!"

"Simple, Neddo," said Roop as he picked up the bookcase and set it against the wall.

"Right," Ned mumbled. "A bloogball. And here you are. Simple." *Aliens*, he thought. *Definitely aliens.*

"And that must be what gave off the really weird signal and pulled us in here," said Suzi, pointing at Ned's communicator.

Ned took another step back. He looked them up and down for terminator guns, antimolecular zappers, and any other alien weapons he could think of. He didn't want to take any chances with these two. One wrong move and they'd probably zap him to powder!

"But where did you come from?" he finally asked.

Roop bit his lip and glanced at Suzi. "Well, Ned," he said, picking up some comic books and cards and stacking them on the desk, "the question isn't *where* we're from. It's more like *when* we're from. And the answer is—the future."

"Yeah, right! You are a real comedian."

Ned laughed. But his laugh trailed off when he saw that Roop wasn't smiling.

"It's no joke, Ned."

Ned backed away even farther. "The *fff—fff*—?" he stuttered. "The *ffff*—?"

"Future," Roop finished. "You know, like, not now, but later?"

"Later?" Ned slumped against the wall. "How much later?"

"The year 2099," said Suzi. "To be exact."

Ned stared at the two of them.

Timehole? The future? 2099?

He flopped down on the bed and groaned. "This isn't happening. Maybe I have gone totally nutzoid like everybody says. Maybe you're some kind of weird dream. Maybe if I blink my eyes you'll both be gone."

He tried it.

It didn't work. They were still there, smiling at him.

Suddenly Roop leaped over to Ned's closet and pulled open the door. He winked and pointed in.

Ned stood up and looked.

There, wedged sideways between un-packed boxes of baseball cards, a slot car track, his science set, cartons of last year's books, and wrinkled school clothes, was—

"A spaceship!"

Suzi peeked over Ned's shoulder. "Actually, it's a hypermodal antigravity warp-class chronoprojection surfer. Surfie, for short."

The little ship had three purple fins sloping up the nose and two longer wings on the side. Under each wing was a yellow jet, blackened at the back.

The surfie reminded Ned of the wild spaceships in his comic books. He touched the shiny surface, running his finger along it.

"It's beautiful!" he whispered. "It looks fast."

"Fast?" Roop beamed. "Suzi, tell him!"

"It's fast," said Suzi. "But right now it's not going anywhere. Can you give us a hand?"

Ned popped his communicator into his back pocket and helped the two kids slide the surfie into his room. It thumped on the floor in the middle of the mess.

Roop started testing the control panel. *Zip-zip!* "Seems okay," he said to Suzi, giving it a quick pat.

"This is totally unbelievable," Ned mumbled. Then it dawned on him. "Wait a second! If you guys are from the future, then you know everything that's going to happen!" He began to pace around the room. "When will I see Ernie again? Will Mr. Smott ever stop frowning and give me an A? Will—"

Suzi shook her head. "Ned . . ."

"Maybe I become world-famous. Do I become world-famous? Or what about my team? How many times do the Indians win the Series?"

"Before or after powerbats?" asked Roop slyly.

"*Powerbats?* Whoa!" cried Ned. "This is excellent! Tell me everything!"

"Sorry," said Suzi. "We can't really tell you much. It wouldn't be right. And we're just starting to learn about traveling in time."

"Yeah," said Roop. "Time is one very

tricky place. If you know something before you're supposed to know it, you could change the course of galactic history!"

Ned snorted. "Hey, I'd settle for a change in just my life."

"Well, maybe there is something about the future that you can get to know right now," Roop said. He tapped a fin on the purple surfie. "What do you say, Neddo? Wanna ride?"

Ned blinked. "Are you kidding? I'd love—" Then he remembered. Slowly he shook his head. "I can't. I mean, I'd better not. I'm in pretty deep trouble with everybody right now."

"Why? What did you do?" asked Roop. He and Suzi sat down on the floor.

"Well, I've got this problem," Ned said, looking at them. "I think maybe I've got a dark side. You know, like I'm loony?"

"Sounds bad," said Suzi.

"*Weird* is the word," said Ned. "Ever since I moved away from my friend Ernie, I've been really out of it. No friends, new school,

that kind of stuff. That's what my mom and dad said, too. Until today."

"What happened?" Suzi asked.

Ned shook his head. "Oh, I just went totally brainless in science class, that's all. I still don't know why. I yelled like this—*Ahhhh!*—and ran out. Everybody was laughing at me. Later Mr. Smott found me in the cafeteria with a big soup pot on my head."

"Definite fashion statement," said Roop, nodding.

Suzi leaned over and flicked a switch on the surfie's control panel. The engines began to hum quietly. "Ned, maybe you need to see your friend again."

"I wish. Ernie lives a thousand miles from here. That way!" Ned pointed out the window and over the trees. "Ohio."

Roop began to smile. "Hey, it's like we told you. This surfie is *fast*. Besides, no one will miss you. Because you won't be gone!"

Ned looked at him, then at Suzi. "What do you mean, I won't be gone?"

"Simple," said Roop. "First we visit your

friend, then we slip into a timehole, punch in some numbers, and—bingo! You're back, even before you left. That's what timeholes are all about."

"Bingo?" Ned repeated.

"Space bingo," said Roop.

"It sounds strange, I know," said Suzi. "Especially to someone in the twentieth century."

"Of course, we have to get the space and time coordinates just right," added Roop. "Or—"

"Or what?" asked Ned.

Roop smiled and patted one of the seats. "Just trust us."

Ned began to smile, too. And that was something he hadn't done in a long time. "Well, maybe a short ride . . ."

"That's my man!" Roop yelped. "Suzi, prepare to party!"

Ned slid into the cockpit behind Suzi and Roop. *WHOOSH!* The engines started up, and the whole house rumbled as if blasted by thunder.

"Ned!" shouted his father.

"What is going *on*?" screamed his mother.

"Uh-oh," Ned gasped as the house started to quake.

An instant later his parents were storming up the stairs to his door. Their footsteps were getting louder and louder. The door-knob started to turn.

Suzi pulled back on the control wheel and a white flame thrust back from the engines, throwing the desk flat against the door and jamming it shut.

"Ohhhhh!" Ned gasped again as the surfie lifted gently off the floor and smoothly glided out his bedroom window.

CHAPTER
3

It was twilight in the sky over Ned's backyard.

"Hold on, everybody!" Suzi said over her shoulder.

VOOOOM! roared the engines behind them.

Ned grabbed his seat as the little spaceship cleared the roof, banked around, and sailed past his bedroom window. He looked in.

It was still a mess. His parents were starting to push the door open. And there he was, flying away in a spaceship.

Yep, he was in trouble again.

But somehow it didn't seem to matter.

"This is unbelievable!" he whispered as the surfie pulled quickly away from the house and shot up into the sky.

Suzi grinned. "Surfies are standard kid equipment in 2099, Ned. Like airbikes and speed shoes."

Roop pointed to his feet. Sleek blue shoes blinked yellow and green. Tiny black jets sprouted from each side.

Speed shoes? thought Ned. Boy, he could have used a pair of those today. To blast far away from school. "But how do you travel in time?"

A quick pull up on the control wheel and Suzi leveled the surfie out. "There are holes in space that loop around. They're hard to find, but you can go in one end and come out the other in a different time and place. They're called timeholes. You've got one in your closet."

"And that little black box you made sends some kind of crazy signal," said Roop. "It opened the timehole and pulled us in."

"Weird," said Ned.

"Weird, yes," said Roop. "But excellent. Suzi and I have just started testing how timeholes work."

The surfie skimmed over the big oak on Ned's corner.

"We'll be flying at tree level for a while," said Suzi. "We usually cruise the ground, but I don't want to attract attention."

"Good idea," said Ned. "I don't think they get too many rockets buzzing around Lakewood."

Roop nudged Suzi. "Hey, that was almost a joke. Ned must be feeling better!"

Ned nodded as the surfie whistled over the treetops that ran along Cedar Road. His road, now.

"So what's it like? The future, I mean."

"It's incredible, it's amazing, it's terrific!" yelled Roop. "And the best part is—kids rule!"

"Kids? Really?"

"Yes. Well, sort of," said Suzi. "Adults do stuff, too, of course. But kids do just about

everything. All that started a few years ago, when we got together and decided to change the bad things."

"Yeah," Roop added, pushing up his glasses, "a couple billion kids can do a lot."

Suzi swung the surfie up over Lakewood Park. "Roop and I are part of a special action team." She tapped a little gold pin on her silver suit. "We're called—"

"Time Surfers!" sang Roop. Then he dropped his voice. "The Time Surfer mission is, one, to help people. Two, to keep the galaxy healthy. Three, to have fun wherever we go."

"That last one is Roop's specialty," said Suzi. Roop turned and grinned.

"Cool," said Ned. He sat back and watched them working the surfie controls. *These two are pretty neat*, he thought. *I wonder if . . .*

Suzi turned the wheel and looped around, heading west. "We'll jump into overdrive in thirty seconds. Next stop, Ernie."

Ned glanced back into the darkening sky behind them. "And you're sure you can get

me back at the exact time and place I just left—my house, seven o'clock?"

"No prob," Roop said. "As long as we don't get hit by another bloogball."

"Oh yeah," said Ned. "And just what is a bloog—"

Zwee-zwee-zwee! A high-pitched siren screeched out from the control panel.

"What's that?" cried Ned.

Roop shot a glance at Suzi. He looked serious now. "Spider Base. Code 3. They need us. I'll activate the TH scanner."

"What's wrong?" asked Ned.

"Quick, Sooz," instructed Roop. "I'm punching in A4-Q7-X9. Better plan a negative approach to Timehole 24."

"We'll have to bank it in," she answered, swinging the surfie around a clump of trees.

"Will someone tell me where we're going?" Ned begged. *"Please?"*

"There!" Roop shouted, pointing to a dark circle between two rocks. The surfie dived for it.

"There?" yelled Ned. They shot down

through the trees. "Where's *there*?"

"Back, Ned. We're going back!"

"To my house?"

"Nope. To ours!"

A second later Suzi yanked the wheel grip, the air crackled, and they disappeared into the silvery blue darkness of a timehole!

CHAPTER 4

Whooooooooooom!

The surfie looped and banked through the timehole tunnel like a roller coaster.

Or a plane spinning out of control.

Or a megatwister slingshot water slide.

Or a—

"Oooh," groaned Ned. "I'm gonna be sick!"

Suddenly the surfie shot around a curve and—*flump!*—popped out the end of the timehole.

Ned's eyes went wide and he swallowed hard. Below him lay an enormous city. It glittered with thousands of colored lights, twinkling in the nighttime sky.

"Are we in . . . I mean, is this still . . . Earth?"

Roop turned around and smiled at Ned. "Posilutely, Neddo. We're flying over Mega City. Feast your eyes on the future!"

Ned looked over the side. There, gleaming under white and blue lights, was something he knew. He gulped. "That's the Statue of Lib—"

Diddle-iddle-eep! Eep! Suddenly the surfie started bumping around.

"Whoa!" shouted Suzi, holding tight to the control wheel as the ship dipped and veered left. "What's going on?"

Eep-eep!

"Yikes!" cried Ned. He quickly grabbed his communicator from his back pocket.

"That crazy signal!" shouted Roop. "Shut it off, quick!"

Ned hit a button on the box and instantly the beeping stopped and the ride smoothed out. "Sorry," he said. "Did I almost kill us all?"

Suzi pulled the surfie back up and quickly

tapped some numbers into its computer. "No, it's okay. But be careful with that in timeholes. Your little black box does some pretty strange things!"

The surfie glided down and slipped neatly between two tall towers. Ned couldn't believe his eyes.

Below him buildings of all different colors twinkled and glowed. Some had long silver arches circling up the sides. "Incredible," Ned whispered.

"Yeah, Mega City is incredible, all right," said Roop, cutting power to the engines. "It's also home."

That's when Ned saw it. A shining ring of blue lights on the ground just below them. Suzi headed toward it.

"That's Spider Base," said Roop. "Time Surfer headquarters. It's a combination school and space command center."

It did look like a spider. One big dome in the middle and eight skinny corridors that jutted out like legs from the center.

"Hangar Pod 5 is free," announced Suzi.

A couple of seconds later, the surfie swooped into the hangar and Roop leaped out. "We'll get you home as soon as we can," he told Ned. "But first we've got to check in at the dome."

Ned and Suzi climbed out and broke into a quick trot behind Roop. They headed down a long corridor. Ned guessed it connected to the big Spider Base dome.

Along the way they ran past some other kids in shiny suits of all different colors. Most of them were carrying strange blinking equipment. Ned had never seen anything like it before. Crazy gadgets with funny-looking pipes and valves and coils.

"It's like a scene out of one of my comic books," he breathed.

"Comic books!" said Suzi with a laugh. "These kids are all working on a special science project."

"Really?" asked Ned. "What are they making?"

"A super surfie, for deep-space travel."

Ned stopped.

Roop laughed. "Hey, it's like we said, Neddo. Kids do everything!"

All the people in the hall smiled at Ned as they passed. Some gave him that funny little wave that Roop had done back in Ned's room.

"Um . . . sorry," Ned said. "I'm not a Time Surfer."

"That doesn't matter," said Suzi, making a funny face. "Anybody can do a snap wave. It's easy. Watch."

Roop and Suzi both snapped their fingers and then quickly raised their hands in a "Hi" motion.

Ned tried it out when a girl in a shiny green suit walked by. The girl smiled and returned the wave.

"See, Ned?" said Suzi. "You're fitting in already."

"Yeah, except for the funny old clothes!" Roop laughed, pointing at Ned.

Ned stopped to look at himself in the shiny wall of the corridor. T-shirt. Jeans. Sneakers. His favorite Indians cap. He

frowned. "What do you mean, funny old—"

Just then a voice echoed through the hall.

"Commander Johnson, report to the dome."

Roop jumped into the air. "Come on, crew, that's us."

"Wow! You're a commander?" Ned asked as they ran.

Suzi laughed. "Him? No way. Not yet. But his mom is! She's a TS teacher. You'll meet her in a minute."

Just ahead of them a gray metal door was starting to slide down.

"Watch this!" cried Roop. He bent down and flicked a lever on each shoe. Tiny blasts of flame shot back. Then he took off for the closing door at top speed. *Shoom!* He jetted along, dropped to the floor, and skidded underneath the door just before it closed with a thud.

"Cool!" said Ned.

"Except sometimes Roop gets totally bageled when the door moves faster than he does!" Suzi told him.

"Totally *bageled*?" said Ned.

The door whisked up and there was Roop. "Not bad, huh?"

"I want to try it," said Ned excitedly. He started running toward the next door.

"Whoa, Ned! Not that one!"

But it was too late.

Ned tore down the hall, skidded along the floor, and slid under the next closing door just in time to see a giant glowing rock hurtling down through the ceiling at tremendous speed.

"AHHHHHHHHHH!" he screamed. It was headed straight for him!

CHAPTER
5

Click!

The giant rock vanished. The ceiling went blue. The lights went up in the huge domed room, and about a hundred kids turned to look at Ned.

He was on the floor.

With his hands over his head.

"Um . . . everybody?" said Roop. "Meet Ned. He's from the past."

"Wow, the past," the kids whispered to each other. They looked at Ned like he was some kind of specimen or something.

Terrific, thought Ned as he looked around. *A classroom. And of course I've got to*

scream. Nedthenerd strikes again.

Everyone in the dome rose and gave Ned a snap wave. He stood up slowly and smiled. He just knew his face was bright red.

A woman stepped down from a control platform in the center of the dome and walked over. "Welcome to the future, Ned. I'm Commander Johnson, Roop's mother."

She wore a white flight suit with sparkles running up and down the arms. "All this must seem strange to you," she said, extending her hand. "And to us, too. You're one of our first visitors from the past."

"It does seem a little strange," said Ned, shaking her hand. Then he looked up at the blue ceiling of the dome. "Well, okay, maybe a lot strange."

"What you saw was a virtual-reality hologram. It seems very real, doesn't it?"

Ned nodded. "Really real. Kind of scary."

Commander Johnson smiled. "This dome is the center of the Time Surfer learning laboratory. Let me show you what we're working on."

She led the three kids over to the control stand and flipped a switch. Instantly the picture came to life again.

"Our space probes in Omega Sector sent us these pictures a little while ago."

Ned looked closer. It was a huge rough rock. A long white tail flowed from the back of it.

"A comet?" he offered.

"That's right," the commander said. "It's made of ice and planetary rock and it's traveling through space at over forty miles a second."

"Zommo!" gasped Roop. "That's fast!"

"Quite fast, Roop," she went on. "It could hit one of the planets in our solar system, so we're watching it very closely."

"What would happen if it hit?" Ned asked.

"Smush City!" cried Roop. "Total Splatsville! Like when a comet crash-landed on Earth about sixty-five million years ago. It's what might have killed the dinosaurs."

Suddenly Ned shuddered. He blinked. His legs went weak. He felt as if someone had

just knocked him on the head.

Dinosaurs? he thought. *Dinosaurs! What is so strange about that word?* He'd heard it a thousand times. He'd even heard it . . . that's it! He'd heard it in school today! Just before he . . .

"What would you do, Ned?"

Ned slowly came out of his daze. "Excuse me?"

"If the comet were going to hit the earth, what would you do to stop it?" asked Commander Johnson.

Everyone in the dome looked at Ned. He could see Suzi smiling, waiting for him to answer. He thought about the question for a while. He tried to remember all the science magazines and comic books he'd ever read.

"Well," he said slowly, "maybe you could shoot some kind of megablaster thing . . ."

"Space cannon?" Suzi suggested.

"Yeah, a space cannon," said Ned. "With a huge missile in it. The blast would push the

comet out of the way. It would just go off into space and wouldn't hit us."

"Good answer," said Suzi.

Commander Johnson looked thoughtful. "That is why we listen to kids, Ned. What you've said is very interesting. Our experts are working on the problem. I'll tell them your idea right now."

Commander Johnson dismissed the class immediately and hurried off down the corridor.

Ned turned to Suzi and Roop. "Boy, I like it here. People really do listen!"

"Told ya," said Roop. "Grown-ups are pretty cool about that."

"Grown-ups? Oh no!" Ned cried. "If we don't get me back, my parents will go nuts wondering where I am."

"Nuts?" said Suzi, puzzled. "I think you mean bagel. Don't you?"

Ned shrugged. "Sure. Whatever."

"Right," said Suzi. She turned to Roop. "Let's get the travel pod ready."

But Roop was shaking his head. "No way, Sooz. Somebody said nuts and my stomach says EAT! Besides, we can't let the kid travel back a hundred years on an empty stomach. Gotta download some chow!"

Suzi turned to Ned.

He shrugged. "Well, I . . ."

"See?" said Roop. "He's so starving he can't compute. Let's recharge!" Roop started trotting toward the kitchen corridor. "Follow me."

"Wait a nanominute," said Suzi. "I have a better idea." She pointed to Roop. "You get the snacks. Ned and I will go to the launch room and warm up the pod."

Roop smiled. "Cool. That way I can make myself a double!" He raced down the corridor, dropped to his knees, and began to slide.

"Does he ever go through a door the right way?" asked Ned as Roop disappeared under a closing door.

Suzi shook her head slowly. "Nope," she

said. "Never." Then she smiled. "But he's a good friend and the absolute best partner on a mission."

"Yeah," said Ned. "I know what you mean. I used to have a friend like that."

CHAPTER 6

"Sorry I screamed back there in the dome," Ned said as he and Suzi entered a round silver room. "I was just being brainless again. I told you I have a loony side."

"I don't think so," said Suzi. "The comet movie scared you. You weren't expecting it."

"That's for sure," Ned mumbled.

"I'm sorry we don't have time to visit your friend Ernie," said Suzi. "But we're needed here."

"It's okay," Ned told her.

In the center of the room sat a clear plastic bubble. The travel pod. It was about five feet high and stood between two green,

blinking columns. Suzi tapped the bubble.

"We use these pods for quick time hops. I'll program everything. All you do is sit and enjoy the ride."

Ned nodded. Inside the bubble was a low seat with a headrest. It looked comfortable.

"I've been thinking, Ned," Suzi said. "Maybe something scared you in school, too. Something you didn't expect." She opened a small hatch on the side of the bubble and began hitting some buttons on a control panel inside. The bubble began to glow.

Ned tried to think about what had happened in school earlier. He couldn't remember much. Something about dinosaurs. And that dumb soup pot on his head. His brain started to hurt just thinking about that. He rubbed his head.

"All I know is I've got to go back there tomorrow and face everybody." He sighed. "Did you ever feel like you can't do anything right? That's how I've felt every day since I moved. I mean—"

Wham!

Something hit the launch room's door from the outside. Then someone groaned.

"Guess who?" Suzi said.

The door shot up. There was Roop, rubbing his arm. "Slow door," he said. "Gotta get that fixed." Then he looked at the bundle of snacks he had been carrying. "Uh-oh. Smushed!"

"No problem," said Ned. "I'll eat anything. But what exactly do Time Surfers eat? Weird purple stuff? Or maybe powdered burgers?"

Roop handed Ned a sparkly blue bundle with a red band around it. "Something totally awesome, Nedman."

"Zooble and krell. I love it," said Suzi. "Try it."

Ned pulled back. "Um . . . I don't know. I guess I'm not that hungry," he said, looking at the blue lump.

Roop slowly opened the square wrapper on his snack. "Ahhhh!" he sang cheerfully. "My favorite smell!"

Ned leaned over and sniffed the bundle. "Hey, I know that smell!"

"You've had zooble and krell?" Roop asked, his eyes wide.

Ned laughed. "Are you kidding?" he said, grabbing at it. "This is peanut butter and jelly! You know, pb and j? Peanut butter and jelly is my main food. It's every kid's main food!"

"Really?" said Suzi. "Ours too!"

Roop laughed. "I guess some things don't change. Peanut jelly and butter, huh? Well, the legend lives on!"

"No, it's peanut butter and—"

Zzzzt!

Suzi pushed some buttons on the control panel in the bubble. "Ned, the pod will get you back to the time and place you left."

"Okay," Ned said, nodding slowly.

"Only, if something goes wrong," Roop cautioned between bites, "and you end up in some place and time you already are, don't meet yourself." He took another bite. "It could be bad."

Ned blinked. "Bad? How bad?"

Roop swallowed. "So bad we call it the

Zonk Zone. Because when there are two of you in the same time and place, one of you gets zonked."

"Zonk Zone?" mumbled Ned. "Doesn't sound too good."

"Ish not," Roop said, licking a small blob of krell off his lip. "Energy explosion. Total wipeout." He chomped into his second sandwich. "It's like this—Ned plus Ned equals KABOOM!"

"Kaboom?" Ned stopped chewing.

"Well, we don't know for sure," said Suzi. "But let's not find out. Time travel is very tricky. And the Zonk Zone is even trickier. Who knows, you might meet Vorg there." She tapped the last numbers and letters into the pod's control panel.

"Umm. Vorg? Who's Vorg?"

"It's a long story," said Roop. "We'll explain it sometime. But right now the pod's ready. Hop in and—bingo! Half a minute, you're home."

"But wait," said Ned as green light coiled and sizzled up the columns on both sides of

the pod. "When can I see you guys again? I mean, maybe we could do something sometime?"

"That would be cool," Roop said excitedly. "We'll definitely arrange it. We'd have an incredible time. Hey—*time!* Get it?"

Ned laughed. Giving his new friends a snap wave, he climbed into the pod. The hatch clamped shut behind him.

It was quiet inside. Ned watched Roop and Suzi work the main controls. Light flooded the room and the pod moved slowly into a round opening in the wall.

So long, guys, thought Ned. *It's been fun.*

An instant later, he was rocketing through the timehole, back into the past.

Back.

To his own time and place.

CHAPTER
7

VOOOOM!

A familiar sick feeling came over Ned as he shot through the tunnel of timeholes. But it wasn't because of the twisting and looping. Not this time.

No. It was the same feeling he'd had when he moved away from Ernie.

Losing friends.

He kept doing that.

Ned looked out of the small pod as it banked through a high turn. There were lots of smaller holes on both sides of the tunnel he was shooting down. He wondered what times and places they went to.

It didn't matter. Pretty soon he'd be back at home. Back at school. Back to his terrible new life. No Ernie. No Suzi or Roop. No friends at all.

Only frowning teachers and screaming sisters and parents who thought he was losing it. Not something to look forward to.

Diddle-iddle-eep!

"Uh-oh!" cried Ned. The pod suddenly jerked up and down in the tunnel.

"My communicator!" screamed Ned.

FLEEE-OOOMP! The pod flipped completely over, spun around in the tunnel, flipped over again, and raced off down a smaller hole on the side.

"HELLLLLLP!" Ned shouted. The pod was rocketing at incredible speed! He grabbed the communicator from his back pocket, felt for the switch, and flicked it off.

The *eep-eeping* stopped. The jerking stopped.

In fact, everything stopped.

The pod skidded to a halt with a sudden jerk.

It was dark. And quiet.

"Oh boy," Ned whispered. "Now I've done it."

He slowly pulled himself out of the pod and felt around in the dark.

A doorknob?

His closet! So it *was* okay. His communicator hadn't messed everything up. He was home.

Ned wondered if he had gotten home at exactly the right time. Or if his parents would be there in his room already, waiting for him. If they'd be mad about the mess. If they'd believe the crazy stuff he'd probably have to tell them.

He pushed on the door. It opened easily.

He saw a shiny linoleum floor.

And a few feet away on the wall, a gray metal box.

A water fountain?

"Uh-oh." Ned's heart raced. "Where am I?"

His floor at home wasn't covered with linoleum. And he sure didn't have a water fountain in his bedroom. The only place they

had this kind of floor and water fountain
was—

The hallway of B-wing.

B-wing of Lakewood School!

"Holy cow!" he shouted.

He looked up at a clock on the wall. 2:00.
"I've messed up big-time."

He was alone in the hall. He listened. Everything was quiet.

Well, not quite everything. Ned could hear
something humming far away. Like a motor
running. Or a person talking.

*Better get out of here before someone sees
me,* he thought. *To the stairs, down, and out
the door. Then, home.*

Ned tiptoed down the hall and peeked
around the corner. Mr. Smott's door was
open. It was his own classroom.

Ned would have to pass the room to get to
the stairs. There was no other way. He
moved out into the hall.

The humming grew louder. It was definitely somebody talking. He could almost
make out what the person was saying. It

seemed like the only sound in the whole school. And it was coming from his classroom.

Then he heard it.

A word.

A single word.

Dinosaurs!

Ned froze. Suddenly he remembered the whole dumb thing in school today.

How he had run from the room tripping over everything and shouting. How Mr. Smott had frowned one of his squish-faced frowns. How everyone else had laughed.

This explained everything. Everything!

Ned began to feel strange all over. His face and hands tingled. His legs felt wobbly.

He knew he shouldn't look in, but he couldn't stop himself. Something was pulling him along. He had to look. He knew what he would see. A boy standing at a desk. Talking to the class.

He knew it because he had been there.

Ned crept up to the classroom and peeked in.

The humming stopped instantly. The boy talking at his desk went silent. He turned to see the face at the door. Ned's face.

And Ned looked at the face of the boy standing in the classroom.

That was Ned's face, too.

"AHHHHHHHHHH!" they both screamed.

Ned tore off down the hall as fast as he could. Right away the other Ned started chasing him.

He remembered it all now! How he had pushed the desks aside and stumbled from the classroom. How he had chased the kid who peeked in when he was talking about dinosaurs.

The kid no one else had seen.

The kid with his face.

Ned blasted through the hall doors and flashed around the corner.

Okay. Maybe I'm not so crazy after all. What are you supposed to do when you see yourself staring at you from the doorway?

Clomp-clomp-clomp! The other Ned was gaining on him. Boy, that kid could run!

Yeah, Ned thought worriedly, *just as fast as I can!* The other Ned was really flying. A few more steps and he'd get him. If only Ned had Roop's speed shoes now!

Ned leaped down the stairs three at a time.

Suddenly the hall doors swung open behind him and the air crackled like a thousand short circuits. Ned felt as if an electric charge was going through him. The closer that other kid—his old self—got, the stranger he felt.

The air was getting hot. And there were . . . sounds. Whispers?

Is this what happens in the Zonk Zone?

The footsteps were flying behind Ned. There was only one chance to get a lead.

Ned took it.

He screeched around a corner, took a flying leap, dropped to his knees, and—*WHAM!* —blasted through a set of double doors and straight into the cafeteria.

CHAPTER
8

It was empty and quiet in the cafeteria. Just Ned alone with the lunch tables and chairs.

Until a second later—*ERRRRRCH!* Footsteps screeched to a stop in the hall just outside.

Ned scrambled across the floor and pushed through a wide silver door into the kitchen. He leaned up flat against the wall and stood there, listening.

The double cafeteria doors swung open with a bang.

Ned didn't move. He could hardly stand. All of a sudden, everything went silent. Ned

felt as if his ears were plugged with cotton. Was it what Suzi had said? Was it . . . Vorg? Ned felt weak and out of breath.

I'm in big trouble now, he thought. *The other me knows I'm in here. He'll find me for sure. Then*—kaboom *and I'm history!*

Erch! Erch! The silence vanished as squeaky sneakers walked slowly through the cafeteria toward the kitchen door.

Ned glanced quickly around the kitchen for places to hide. Oven. Dishwasher. Refrigerator. No good. There wasn't anywhere to go. This was it. He grabbed the only thing near him and stood against the wall.

"Sorry I've got to do this, pal," he whispered. "But it's like Roop said. Ned plus Ned equals—"

The steps came closer. Ned held his breath. The kitchen door began to edge open.

Ned saw a familiar sneaker slowly set itself down on the kitchen floor.

Suddenly—*Clunk! Yeeoww! Crash!* There was a blur of Ned and door and something

shiny that was over in an instant.

And then there was just the door, swinging back and forth on its hinges. And groaning coming from the cafeteria on the other side of the door.

Ned peeked through.

There he was, the other Ned, stumbling into chairs and tables, a huge silver soup pot on his head. The hallway door was just jerking open and Mr. Smott was stepping in, beginning to frown.

"Uh-oh!" Ned whispered. "I've gotta get out of here!"

Suddenly the whole kitchen started humming, and the air began to hiss and crackle. Swirls of light flashed and flickered all around him.

THWAAAANK! The huge aluminum refrigerator door burst open wildly.

"Get in, Ned!" shouted a voice. "The comet! It's heading right for Earth! We need you!"

Ned whirled around to see a face staring at him from between two big pickle jars. He

bent over. "Roop?" he said.

Then Ned saw a puff of white breath rising over a bag of carrots. He bent over some more and squinted at another face. "Suzi?"

"Timeholes are everywhere, Ned," she burst out. "Now hurry!"

Wham! Something—or maybe someone with a pot on his head—slammed against the kitchen door.

Suzi grabbed Ned's hand. And he dived in through the refrigerator over tomorrow's lunch and into the seat of a spaceship roaring away from Lakewood.

"Whoa! Where am I?" asked Ned.

"On a mission," said Suzi. "Strap in."

Ned looked around. It was the surfie, but it was different. Larger. And he was in the control cabin. A wide viewing port ran across the front. On either side of Ned's seat were blinking devices like those he had seen in the hallways of Spider Base.

Roop tapped Ned's arm, then touched a control panel in front of him. Instantly a series of long fins jutted out from the sides and

back of the ship.

"It's the science project, Neddo. Our surfie has been totally customized. It's zommo to the max! Note the excellent Z-wing styling. Isn't it amazing what kids can do?"

Suzi accelerated the ship through a series of lightning-fast turns.

"Listen, guys, you'll never believe—"

"Sorry, Ned, you'll have to save it for later," Suzi interrupted. She frowned. "If there is a later."

"Huh?" gasped Ned.

"Suzi's right," said Roop. "It doesn't look good. That enormous comet took some kind of space bounce, and it's speeding right for Earth!"

The surfie blurred through the silver tunnel and shot out into the sky over Spider Base. "But what can I do? I'm just a regular kid," Ned asked worriedly.

Suddenly a screen on the main control board lit up. Commander Johnson's face appeared.

"Kids," she said, "there's less than an hour

before the comet hits Earth. Our main computer estimates that the impact will cause huge tidal waves and earthquakes all over the world."

Roop shook his head. And Ned saw a tear forming in Suzi's eye. She quickly wiped it away.

Commander Johnson went on. "We don't have time to launch another spacecraft. Your plan, Ned, is our only hope."

Ned stared at the screen. "Excuse me? My plan?"

"To shoot the comet out of the way!" cried Suzi. "I knew it was great when you said it!"

"Right, Neddo," said Roop. "Sooz and I will fly this rig. It'll be your job to punch that ugly rock to never-never land." Roop shoved his fist in the air. "Ka-pow!"

"But . . ." Ned felt a little dizzy. "I mean, doesn't anyone have a better idea?"

"Nope," said Suzi, handing him a space helmet.

"But there's got to be a—"

"Nope," said Roop, snapping a pair of gog-

gles on him. They fit perfectly.

"But—"

VRRRRROOOOOOOOOOM!

The rocket blasted through the open sky, past the clouds, and up into the deep darkness of space!

CHAPTER 9

The sky around the ship seemed immense. Darkness was everywhere. Tiny stars shimmered in every direction.

Ned thought of all the space movies he'd ever seen. All the comic books he'd ever read.

But this was different. This was real. A mission to save Earth from total destruction.

If they could save it. *If* his idea was a good one. *If*—

"Bonka-bonka! Anybody home?" Roop was tapping on Ned's helmet. "Heads up," he said. "We should be seeing that oversized jawbreaker anytime now. Better keep a look-

out for it. See anything?"

Ned scanned the deep black space in front of the ship. "Nothing yet, guys."

Better find that comet and stop it, he thought. *If we don't we're as dead as . . . dinosaurs.*

His brain flashed at the word. He wanted to tell Suzi and Roop about the whole thing in school. But there wasn't time for that now. And there might not be any time later if his plan didn't work. No, he had a job to do. That was the only thing that mattered.

Ned scanned the port again. "Some kind of moon coming into view." He pointed to a big gray shape just entering their viewport.

Suzi looked up from the controls. "There isn't supposed to be any moon here."

"Right there," said Ned. He pointed again to the big chunk of rock moving across the sky.

Roop stared out the front port. He gasped.

"Holy megabloogball—that's no moon!"

An instant later the enormous rock the size of a planet filled the sky in front of the ship.

"Battle stations!" Roop shrieked. "That's one big comet!"

VROOOOOM!

The comet hurtled past the ship at incredible speed.

"Zommo! It's really flying!" said Suzi. "Thrusters—on!" The Z-Wing surfie jolted ahead, slamming all three of the crew back in their seats.

"Okay, plan man," Roop said, whirling around to face Ned. "The space cannon is lowered and in position. It's got a class Q missile on board. And they don't get any better than that. So get ready to slam-dunk that chunk of junk!"

A grip stick swung around in front of Ned. "Okay, you guys," he said. "I'm going to fire this thing."

Suzi gunned the engines and the surfie

zoomed deep into the gassy white tail of the comet. They were gaining on it.

"Ready," said Ned as he placed his finger on the trigger.

"Aim!" He locked the comet in on the laser range finder.

"Fiiiiii—wait!" He looked up. "I lost it!"

They all stared out the front viewport.

Nothing. No comet.

"Lost it?" cried Suzi. "How could we lose something the size of Jupiter? I don't get it."

Roop scanned the darkness in front of them. "This is weird. First it's there and then it isn't."

The sky was totally empty.

Ned bolted up in his seat. "It's as if . . ." His brain was going at hyperspeed. "That's it!"

"What's it, Nedman?" said Roop. "You know where it went?"

"Wrong question, Roop," said Ned. "Not *where*—but *when*."

Suzi gasped. "You mean—"

"Right," said Ned. "The comet must be in a timehole!"

"Buzzy, quick," Suzi shouted into the control panel. "Where did that comet go?"

The computer whizzed to life. "One moment, please."

Ned's eyes widened. "Your computer talks?"

"I can even sing," said the computer. "But first . . ."

Ned watched as the computer's screen flashed back quickly through the years. Back, back . . .

Then it stopped.

"No! That's my year! The year I live in," Ned moaned.

"I'm sorry," said Buzzy.

Suzi looked over at Roop. "Okay, we know when. Now—where?"

Buzzy got to work again, its screen blurring through a thousand different places. Then it stopped. A place flashed across the screen.

A city.

A street.

A number.

Ned read the flashing screen. "No way! There's got to be a mistake. That's . . . that's . . . Ernie's house!"

CHAPTER 10

"Full power! Extra rockets! Hit the road! Let's move it!" Ned screamed. "Ernie will be smushed if we don't save him!"

Roop stared at the computer screen. "It won't work. The comet will strike Earth in exactly one minute. We're two minutes late. We'll never make it in time."

"No!" cried Ned, looking first at Suzi, then at Roop. "There's got to be a way. We can't just let the world explode! Everybody will be killed. Starting with my best friend!"

He stared at Suzi again, searching her face for some hope. "This can't be happening!" he cried.

Then he slumped down in his seat.

"Yeeoow!"

Ned reached into his back pocket. "Oh, this dumb communicator again. It's always—"

Suddenly it came to him.

"Hey, I've got it!" Ned spun around.

"Got what?" asked Roop.

"My communicator. Remember? It gives out a really strong signal, and it does weird things in timeholes, right?"

"Right, but . . ." Suzi shook her head.

"Ernie's got one, too! If I call him on this, maybe the signal will pull us to his house before the comet gets there."

"Let's gun those engines, Sooz," Roop said. "It's worth a try!"

Suzi jammed the thrusters forward and the Z-wing surfie shot across empty space and into the timehole.

Ned flicked the communicator on and started shouting. "Ernie, come in. This is Ned. Come in, Ernie, come in!"

Roop leaned over. "That thing better work!"

"It'll work," said Ned, "or I don't know my comic books." He twisted a dial on the front of the box. "Now if I can just . . ."

Diddle-iddle-eep! Eep! The communicator began to beep.

The rocket instantly started to buck and wobble in the timehole.

"Yahoo!" cried Roop. "He's got it!"

"Come in, Ernie!" Ned shouted. "Red alert. This is the real thing, buddy!"

He waited for a sound.

Suddenly the speaker crackled. "Ned?" said a sleepy voice. "Is that you?"

Ned jumped up and down in his seat. "Yippee! It's Ernie!"

"Hey," Ernie's voice crackled. "Do you know what time it is?"

"Trick question, Ern. I'll explain it all later. For now, just keep your communicator on and stay under the covers."

"Yeah, well, okay," Ernie yawned.

Suzi leaned into the controls. The surfie bumped up and down like a sled on rocks. "Ned, if we can keep the signal open we should be able to—*whoa!*"

Suddenly the ship flipped end over end a half dozen times and shot off sideways into a small tunnel.

"Thirty seconds to impact," Buzzy announced.

"Pour it on, Suzi!" yelled Roop, holding onto his seat.

"I'm pouring!" Suzi hit the overdrive switches and—*whoosh!*—the rocket blurred through one tunnel after another.

The communicator was heating up in Ned's hand. "Hold on, Ernie. We're on our way!" A second later they popped out of the timehole—and blasted into Ernie's bedroom!

"AHHHHHHHHH!"

Ernie was standing on his bed in his pajamas, screaming at the top of his lungs as the spaceship shot sideways from his closet and

flashed through his room.

"*AHHHHHHH!*" Ernie screamed again.

Ned tried to wave to him but the surfie bolted out an open window and into the night before he had a chance.

"Bingo!" shouted Roop. "We made it in time! We got to the right place and time. But where is the—"

RRRROOOOOMMMMM!

The whole sky thundered around them.

"There!" shouted Ned. "Above us!"

It was there, all right. The huge icy rock was tumbling toward Earth at incredible speed. The air boomed and roared.

"Ten seconds!" cried Suzi.

"Blast it, Ned. It's all up to you!" Roop shouted, squeezing Ned's shoulder.

Ned grabbed the firing arm and brought the laser cannon into position.

"Five seconds . . ."

He took aim.

"Two seconds!"

He fired.

KA-BLOOOOOM!

The cannon blast ripped through the sky, sending the surfie flipping backward over and over.

The air above Ernie's house turned red, then yellow, then white. The whole sky quaked and rumbled from the explosion. Then everything went quiet.

And the smoke cleared.

The comet was gone.

"He shoots—he scores!" yelled Roop.

Suzi looped the ship around for a better look.

People were coming out of their houses and standing in the street. A thick white haze hung above Ernie Somers's house.

"But where did the comet go?" Suzi asked.

Ned could see Ernie leaning out of his window, staring into the sky. "It went back where it came from, Sooz," Ned said. Then he smiled. "And you know what Roop says—comet plus comet equals—*kaboom!*"

"Ned," gasped Suzi, "you saved the world!"

"What did I tell you?" Roop yelped. "Kids do everything!"

"Now I know what you mean," said Ned.

Suzi flicked on the ship's transmitter. "Spider Base," she said, laughing, "get the purple carpet ready, we're coming in!"

CHAPTER 11

When the door whisked up and Ned stepped into the Spider Base dome, hundreds of people began to applaud, nodding their appreciation. Brightly colored globes of light floated freely above the crowd, and a rock band began to blast out a song.

Ned looked at Suzi and Roop. Their faces were beaming.

"It's for you, Nedman. You're the hero here. And look—they've managed to find a band that still does rock!" Roop laughed. "Rock! My grandpa told me about it."

"But . . ."

"No buts, Ned." Suzi smiled. "We're right

behind you." She nudged him over to a stage in the middle of the dome.

Roop's and Suzi's parents were there with lots of other grown-ups. They all wore fancy shiny suits. Commander Johnson stepped over to Ned. The music swelled and stopped.

"Ned Banks," she announced. "On behalf of all of us, please accept this medal as a token of our thanks." She leaned over and pinned a small gold pin on Ned's T-shirt.

It had letters on it. *TS.* And a lightning bolt. It was just like the pins Suzi and Roop wore.

"But . . ."

"Yes, Ned, we are proud to welcome you as an official Time Surfer. You are hereby assigned to TS Squad One!"

Everyone in the dome started clapping and cheering. Applause filled the room. The band started rocking and rolling again.

"We're really glad to have you on the team," said Suzi, giving Ned a quick hug.

"Yeah," said Roop as he poked Ned. "Totally zommo for a kid from the past, huh?"

Suddenly Ned remembered. "The past? Bagel, we've got to get me home!"

"That's definitely a mission for the Time Surfers!" said Suzi.

* * *

The surfie pulled in its fins and slid to a stop just inside Ned's closet. By the glow of the timehole, Ned could easily make out the boxes of his junk piled all around them.

"Time Surfer," Ned said as he hopped out of the surfie onto the closet floor. "I like the sound of that. Ernie will never believe it."

"Oh," said Roop. "That reminds me. I've got something for you." He popped open a compartment on the surfie's control panel and took something out. He handed it to Ned.

"My communicator! I thought I lost it in the explosion." *It looks different*, Ned thought.

"Roop really souped it up," said Suzi. "If you ever need to find a timehole, just press this green button. The blue button calls us."

"Cool! What's the yellow button for?"

Suzi looked at Roop. They smiled at each other. "That's a surprise. Try it when we leave."

"Thanks," Ned told them. "You know, today has been really fun."

Suzi patted him on the arm. "Not to mention exciting!"

The three Time Surfers gave each other a snap wave.

"See you later, Neddo," said Roop. "Get it? Later. As in the future?" He cracked up. "Maybe we can play a game of bloogball, just the three of us?"

Ned was just about to ask for the millionth time what a bloogball was, but the engines rumbled and the purple surfie disappeared into the shimmering blue of the timehole.

Ned knew what was waiting for him on the other side of the closet door. His messy room. His messy life. School.

Still, things weren't *so* bad. He'd had *some* adventure, that was for sure. "A surprise, huh?" he said, holding up the communicator.

Slowly he pressed the yellow button.

Suddenly the air in his closet swirled and flashed. And before Ned knew it—

OOOOMMPH! From out of nowhere came a dark shape! It plowed into him, knocking him into a carton of old school papers and report cards.

"Ouch!" said a sleepy voice from the floor.

It couldn't be!

"Ernie?" whispered Ned. He opened the door slightly to get some more light.

The shape next to him sat up. "Ned?"

"Ernie!"

"Um . . ." Ernie looked into the deep tunnel on one side, then at the junk in Ned's closet on the other. "Where did I . . . I mean, how did you . . . I mean . . . oh brother, I must be dreaming!"

Ned shifted over next to Ernie on the closet floor and started to explain everything.

* * *

"And that's what happened," he finished,

taking a deep breath and looking at Ernie.

Ernie's mouth had dropped open. "So it's not a dream?" he whispered.

"Nope. It really happened. It's still happening. And it's all because of this." Ned held up the communicator. "This little box just happens to locate timeholes."

"Wow."

"Yep. And the way I see it, our problems are solved."

"How?" Ernie whispered again.

"Don't you get it?" said Ned. *"Both* our houses have timeholes. We can spend all day here, then go to your house and spend all day there. We can have two whole lifetimes of fun!"

Ernie nodded slowly. Then he started to grin a big, long grin.

"But listen," Ned said. "There's one thing I've been thinking about. I don't think we can tell anybody. Not right away."

Ernie laughed. "Hey, who would believe us anyway? *Timeholes? The future?* It sounds like a Zontar comic!"

Ned laughed, too. He grabbed Ernie's hand. They locked their thumbs tight. "Secret?" said Ned.

"Secret," said Ernie. "Boy, this is going to be excellent. Just like the old days."

"Yeah, but we'll have to do a lot of testing first. There's this wicked place called the Zonk Zone. Very weird. And very dangerous. And I think there's something or someone called Vorg who lives there."

"Sounds cool." Ernie grinned again. Then he yawned. "So see you tomorrow?"

"Absolutely!" said Ned, smiling. He gave Ernie a snap wave, pressed the yellow button again, and—

WHOOSH!—the whole house rumbled as if blasted by thunder. Ernie flashed one way into the timehole and Ned tumbled the other way, out of the closet and onto his bedroom floor.

"Ned!" shouted his father.

"What is going *on* up there?" screamed his mother.

An instant later Ned's parents were storm-

ing up to his room. The knob was starting to turn—

That's when it hit him.

All this happened before!

He looked at the clock on his bookshelf. 7:00 P.M.!

He'd done it. Just as Roop had promised. He'd actually come back before he'd left!

Ned quickly pulled the desk and the other junk away from the door. It swung open and Ned's parents stepped into the room.

"Oh!" his mother gasped in horror.

His father carefully picked his way over the clothes and books that lay scattered on the floor. He stood the desk chair back on its legs. "It looks like the end of the world in here!"

"End of the world? Well, almost, Dad, but it could have been a lot worse."

"I don't see how," his mother said. Ned could tell she was annoyed. "Before you go to bed, I want this room picked up. And you can spend some time working on your closet, too." She ruffled his hair. "I mean it."

Ned brightened. "Really? The closet? Sounds great, Mom. I'd love to."

"Are you feeling okay?" his father asked, feeling his forehead.

"I'm fine."

"Strange," his father murmured, tiptoeing over the stray comic books. "Good night, Ned."

*   *   *

After his parents left, Ned cleaned up and put everything away. Things were going to be all right. The day had started out pretty bad. But it had ended with him saving the planet. That was good. And he'd made a couple of incredible new friends—even if they did live about a hundred years in the future. That was good, too.

Best of all, he could see Ernie anytime he wanted. Just by opening his closet door.

He would still have to face the kids in his class tomorrow. And Mr. Smott. But things would be okay. In fact, the future looked pretty—

KAAAA-FLOOOOOOOOOOM!

Ned's closet door blew open.

Roop shot right across Ned's desk and into his bookcase. A second later, Suzi slammed into the far wall. Comic books went flying all over the place. The room was an instant mess.

"Time Surfer alert!" yelled Suzi.

"Pack your bags!" cried Roop. "We're on a mission!"

Yeah, thought Ned, grinning. *The future.*

It was going to be fun.